Jay and the Old Big Blue Truck

Author LAURIE HURT

Illustrator NATASHA PARKER

To order additional copies of this book, contact:
Xlibris
844-714-8691
www.Xlibris.com
Orders@Xlibris.com

ISBN: Softcover   978-1-4363-5487-5
           Hardcover   978-1-4363-5488-2
           EBook   978-1-6641-8512-8

Library of Congress Control Number: 2008905925

Print information available on the last page

Rev. date: 07/13/2021

TABLE OF CONTENTS

DEDICATION

This children book" Jay and the Old Big Blue Truck" is dedicated first to God, and then to my husband, Wiley, his brothers, Henry, David, John, and wife Deborah, our sons, Carlos and Chris their friends, LaShell and Stephanie, Lisa and Bonnie and to my parents, George and Alcora, my sister, Lenora, my brother, Elvis, and his wife, Sherease. Also, this is dedicated to Eleanor, and my deceased brother, George E.

SPECIAL DEDICATION TO MY GRANDCHILDRENS, UNCLES, AUNTS, NEICES, NEPHEWS, COUSINS, FRIENDS, and NEIGHBORS

Special Acknowledgments To:

Minister-Laura Carey
Minister- Patricia A. Hogue

Pastor and Mrs. J W. Hunt of New Covenant Fellowship
Church of God, Lynchburg, Virginia.

Paul and Maria Mitchell
John and Ellen Newbill
Dottie Smith
Doug and Sharon Nelms
Odessa Flood
Roberta Kasey
Carlos Hurt
Christopher Hurt

Pastor and Mrs. J. Waller of Mt Olivet Missionary Church
Bedford, Virginia

Lee Walker-WTOY-Radio Station, Roanoke, VA

Dr. Marvin McGinnis-Principle of Body Camp Elementary School
Bedford, Virginia

Who has given me the confidents and has helped me in sponsoring my previous book, entitled.
"What I Think I Want To Be"

Now Special Acknowledgements To:

Natasha Parker-Illustrator-Bedford, Virginia
Wil Clay-Author - Illustrator of Children's Books and Storyteller- Toledo, Ohio

Tab 0 'Neal- producer and talk show host of Living in the Heart of Virginia — WSET-TV
Lynchburg, Virginia

Charlotte Maxey
Janet Mills
Viola Henry
Tracy Young
Mildred Yarbrough
Michelle Patterson
Evelyn Thomas

With their encouragement, I have now published "Jay and the Old Big Blue Truck"

Chapter 1

Jay's Surprise

"Momma, what am I going to do for the summer?" asked Jay. Jay's Momma knew how active he was. She knew that he had to be doing something. Jay knew that summer was the time that he would not be around his school friends. As time drew near for school to close for the summer, the more depressed Jay was feeling. Jay had hoped to have a very exciting summer at his grandparents' house.

Jay's plans were to spend summer with his Papa and his Grandma in the country. He wanted to have fun playing with the cat named Static and the old, big, brown dog called Tic at his grandparent's house. But most of all Jay could not wait to help his Papa. Jay knew that Papa was always doing something and staying busy. Jay knew that Papa could also use another hand. Although Jay was seven, he had the mind of an adult when work had to be done. Jay would stop playing instantly just to help Papa with his work.

In the city Jay knew that it would be impossible to have any fun if he had to stay with someone else, like old Mrs. Skylinskey. Mrs. Skylinskey lived three doors down from Jay's apartment complex. Mrs. Skylinskey kept children for the summer while their parents worked. Staying with old Mrs. Skylinskey was boring to Jay, because he loved the outdoors. With Mrs. Skylinskey he could only stay outside for certain periods of time. Mrs. Skylinskey would have not only children Jay's age, but she kept much smaller ones too. Even though Mrs. Skylinskey was a very good cook, Jay wanted more. Jay wanted to be with his grandparents. Jay knew that his Grandma could really throw down some biscuits that were tummy-aching delicious, each time you bit into one. But Jay had to think how he could get his plan to work.

Jay's only hope was to have his Papa and Grandma to call, and talk to his Momma to see if they would like for him to come and spend the summer with them. But, would Papa and Grandma think of asking his Momma that question, if they called her? Jay did not know how he could make this happen.

Living in the city was sometimes boring to Jay. Jay loved playing with his friends. He wanted to go outside everyday to play, but in the city it was not safe for a child to be out alone. Jay's Momma would at times after work, pick up Jay and his friends from school and take them to the park, or the Dairy Queen or skating. Sometimes Jay would come from school and be stuck inside all evening.

But surprisingly without Jay knowing, Jay's Papa and Grandma had called his Momma. They had called to invite him to come and stay with them in the country for the summer. His grandparents

knew that school would be over soon. Jay's Momma was very happy his grandparents had called to invite him. Jay's Momma told his grandparents that it would be great for him to come and stay for the summer. Jay's Momma told his grandmother that Jay needed this time away for the summer, because his Dad had left this week for a one year tour of duty in Iraq. Jay knowing that his Dad was gone for a year made him sad. Jay loved his Dad so much that he did not want him to go.

Jay had also worked hard this year in school, he had received many certificates this year, one for perfect attendance, one for being the best in his math class,and for assisting the teacher, that Jay's Momma wanted to surprise him about this year's summer plans.

Jay slowly came in the room where his Momma was sitting in a recliner. He flopped down on the couch playing with his Game Boy.

Jay had such a strong and serious look on his face, his Momma was worried, so she asked him what was upsetting him. He had a frown one inch deep on his face. It looked like a map from north to the south, instead of being straight his frown was wobbly. Jay seriously asked his Momma again what he would be doing this summer? Jay started gritting his teeth because he was uncertain of what his Momma might say to him. He did not want to hear his Momma say, well, you will have to stay with Mrs. Skylinskey. He wanted to hear something else that involved Papa and Grandma. Would Mom say what with Jay was really hoping to hear?

Finally, Jay's Momma told him after dinner that Papa and Grandma called. Jay was very excited, now, Jay was wondering, what had they talked about? Did they talked on the subject of summer vacation for him or what? Then with a long pause, Mom surprisingly said to Jay, "They wanted to invite you to the country for the summer." Jay jumped sky high.

"What did you say, Momma? What did you tell them? "I told them that it would be great for you to come."

"Whee, I get to go to Papa and Grandma's for the summer," exclaimed Jay. Jay was concerned about his Momma being alone, but she assured him that she would be all right. Jay's Momma told him to go and have fun, just keep in touch by calling. Jay's Momma told him that she had a lot to do around the house, along with working everyday.

Jay could not wait for school to be over. He went to his room and started packing. Jay packed his football, basketball, skates, baseball bat and then some of his clothes. Jay loved his Grandma, but loved Papa more. School finally was out so Jay was on his way to stay with his grandparents.

Jay loved the outdoors and loved riding in the old, big, blue truck of Papa's, coming to visit with his grandparents meant a lot to him. Jay arrived at his Papa and Grandma's house late in the evening. Jay saw Papa cutting up wood and stacking the wood. Jay wanted very much to help. Jay gave his Grandma and Papa big hugs and kisses and then rushed

upstairs to change his clothes. Jay did not want to mess up his nice clothes that his Momma had bought him.

When Papa saw Jay coming to help, Papa moved his wood splitting down farther away from Jay. Papa did not want Jay to get hurt while visiting with them. Papa showed Jay what to do. Jay quickly started helping Papa by picking up the small and large sticks of wood and piling the wood in the shed. Jay stacked the pieces of wood on top of each other in a pattern the way that Papa had shown him. But when Jay stacked the last pile of wood in the shed, a little creature called a skunk surprised Jay. The skunk had scooted his small frame body under the shed from the outside. When Jay saw the skunk, Jay yelled for Papa, "Papa! Papa!" But Papa did not hear Jay the first time. Jay yelled louder, "Papa! Papa!" Jay finally got Papa's attention.

"What is it Jay?" Papa said

Jay yelled, "A skunk!"

Papa yelled louder back to Jay as he was walking towards the shed, "What did you say?"

Jay said again, "A skunk!" As soon as Papa entered the shed, he saw Jay and the skunk. The skunk was looking down at the ground for bugs. Jay was looking at the skunk, hoping not to be sprayed. The skunk saw some bugs over on the other side of the shed. It waddled its way over to the other side. When the skunk moved, Papa grabbed Jay and ran out of the shed. In a flash, Papa had Jay and was heading towards the house as fast as he could run. The skunk did spray Jay and Papa. But as Papa had Jay running out of the shed, they only received a little of the awful smelling odor. When skunks get upset about anything, this is what they do, they spray you," said Papa, since they only receive a little of the skunk spray, Jay and Papa had to bath in tomato juice and then take regular baths several times before the odor would leave the both of them. When Jay and Papa had finished doing all of their bathing, Grandma told Papa and Jay that they would have to sleep outside on the porch, maybe just for a few nights. The porch was screened in, so Grandma was not worried about anything else happening to Jay and Papa. The odor was slowly

fading away. Jay told Papa that this sure is a fine way to start a vacation. Papa looked at Jay and they both laughed and chuckled.

The very next morning, while Jay was outside with Papa, Jay heard his Grandma in the kitchen moving around pots and pans. Grandma was busy cooking breakfast. Grandma wanted to make sure that Jay and Papa had a good breakfast before starting their day. Jay could smell the delicious fried bacon, scrambled eggs and ham and those delicious buttered biscuits. Grandma was going to call Jay and Papa to eat as soon as she put on Papa's coffee. Grandma knew that Jay and Papa were sleeping out on the porch from last night's mishap with the skunk. Soon Grandma called Jay and Papa in for breakfast.

Jay and Papa thanked Grandma for the delicious breakfast. Then Papa went outside working on his old, big, blue truck setting in front of his shop. Papa raised up the hood of the old, big, blue truck. Papa started checking the oil and said that he needed more oil. Jay went into Papa's shop and got a can of Chevron oil that Papa used all the time in his old, big, blue truck. Jay gave the oil to Papa to pour in the old, big, blue truck, then Papa checked the radiator for water. Papa could see that the water was low. Jay took the bucket over to the water spigot. He filled the bucket with water. The bucket of water started swishing in and out as he walked across the yard. Jay's pants had gotten very wet, but Jay did not mind getting wet. Jay gave the bucket of water to Papa to pour into the old, big, blue truck's radiator.

Papa was a tall man with deep, dark, brown eyes and smiled all the time. Papa looked to be in his late 50's and worked hard for a living. Papa knew how hard it was to raise a child in the city. He wanted very much to teach Jay the right values of life. He knew Jay believed and trusted in him.

Then Jay started thinking, "I really would like to go riding in that old, big, blue truck." So he asked, "Papa, Can I go riding with you in the old, big, blue truck today?" Papa had already planned to take Jay riding, but Jay asked him before he could tell him the good news of riding with him to the mill to carry a load of lumber.

Papa told Jay, "Yes! I'm taking a load of lumber to the sawmill today."

Jay shouted, "Oh boy." Jay could not wait to ride in that old, big, blue truck of Papa's. The old, big, blue truck was a 1970's model Chevy with a dumpster, but it was also made to carry lumber for Papa. Papa has had his truck ever since Jay and his cousin Carlashia were born. This old, big, blue truck had the smell of pine, oil and old bark. Jay knew that his Momma wouldn't like the ride or the smell of the old, big, blue truck if she was here to ride in it, but to Jay it meant a lot. It meant that he and Papa had work to do with this old truck. Papa made his living working at the sawmill and logging for his business. Papa would buy the trees from people who owned forest land. Then he would cut the trees down. Sometimes Papa would bring the trees to his mill, then Papa would saw the trees unto different sizes of lumber. Next, Papa would deliver the lumber to a larger mill to make furniture from it. As for Jay this was exciting.

Chapter 2
The Trip to Franklin's Sawmill

Before Papa and Jay could leave, they checked the tires. Papa looked down and saw at a glance that on the left side of his truck was a flat tire. Papa went around the old, big, blue truck to check the other tires. The other tires were fine. Papa found out that he had picked up a nail. Papa went and got a spare tire from the shop. Papa kept a lot of them because he never could tell when the old, big, blue truck would need one. Papa knew that the tire had to be fixed before he could leave for the mill. So Jay went to get Papa the tire tool to loosen the nuts on the wheel. Papa removed the flat tire and put on the good tire. Papa knew they had a long way to travel.

After replacing the tire, Papa was ready to leave. Jay and Papa started on their way to the mill. Jay did not want anything to go wrong on this trip. Jay told Papa to buckle up, so they both buckled their seat belts to be safe on the long trip. Jay thought that this was a good time to let Papa know some of the things that he had learned in school.

Jay and Papa started on their way. As soon as Papa had gone about fifty miles down the road from the house, the old, big, blue truck started sputtering. Jay asked Papa, "What was that noise?" Jay said, "It sounded like the noise was coming from under the hood of the truck." But Papa said that he did not know what the noise could be. Papa pulled far off on the side of the road. Papa lifted up the hood of the truck. Papa saw that a spark plug was causing the trouble. So, while Papa was looking to see which spark plug was causing the sputtering in the truck, Jay jumped out of the truck to watch.

Jay saw that Papa had picked up a wrench, so Jay picked up one too. Papa went to the right side of the truck, while Jay decided to jump up on the left side. Papa was so busy that he paid no attention to Jay

was doing. Jay began turning every screw on his side of the truck. Then suddenly, one of the screws that Jay turned started spewing steam. Jay jumped down and dropped the wrench on the ground. Papa saw the steam coming out. Papa ran to the side of the truck that Jay was on. Papa asked Jay for the wrench, Jay could not find the wrench. The wrench had gone underneath the truck on the other side. Papa went down on his knees looking furiously for the wrench. Papa found the wrench and began turning the screw as fast as he could to stop the steam from coming out. Soon Papa had fixed the hose that Jay had unscrewed with the wrench. Papa told Jay that it was nice to help, but just wait until he can stand from the ground up before he decides to work on the old, big, blue truck again. Papa smiled at Jay, and went back to finish the problem that he was working on. Jay with a very sad face told his Papa that he was sorry. Jay was worried that Papa would not ask him along on any other trip. For Jay, that was a question for Papa to answer.

Jay then decided to pick up gravel along the roadside and pitch them into the ditch. As Jay was pitching the gravel he walked a little ways off from the truck. All of a sudden, Jay saw something black that was shining, It looked like a shining 5-inch long rope lying in the path where Jay was walking. Jay stepped closer to the shining long rope and found it to be a shining, black, baby snake. When the snake saw Jay, it was just as frightened of Jay than Jay was of it. Jay took off running back to Papa's truck and the snake hastily slithered away. Jay opened the door of the truck and flew inside. Jay stayed in the truck until Papa fixed the

problem with the old, big, blue truck. From inside of the truck, Jay told Papa about the baby snake and what he and the snake did to get away from each other. Papa looked at Jay and laughed and told Jay to always watch where he is stepping. Papa said to Jay that this could have been a big problem if the snake had been poisonous and had decided to strike.

Soon Papa had completed working on the old, big, blue truck. Papa started the truck and it sounded perfect. No more sputtering, and no more steam did the old, big, blue truck make.

When things had settled down, Jay asked Papa, "How far is this mill that we're riding to?" Papa told Jay it was just about as far as he lived from the country. Jay asked Papa, "How far is that?" Papa laughed at him. Papa told Jay that he was going to Franklin's Sawmill. The mill was now about ten miles away,and Papa told Jay that they were almost there. Papa wanted to let Jay know that this is where lumber is sold. The sawmill uses this lumber to make furniture and to build all types of houses.

Papa asked Jay if he could name some furniture made of wood. Jay answered and told Papa that he could. He started naming chairs, tables, desks and picture frames and much more that was made of wood. Papa said to Jay, "You are right, that is very good. You have passed my test."

With Jay riding along, Papa did not need a radio in the truck. Jay talked and asked questions all the way. Jay asked Papa, "Will we see large machines at the mill? Will bigger trucks be coming in and out of the mill? How long does it take to unload a truck?" Jay was so excited to be on this trip with Papa. Papa did not want to answer any of Jay's questions yet. Papa wanted Jay to see and find out for himself when they arrived at Franklin's Sawmill.

Chapter 3
Near Accident

Jay and Papa continued on their way to Franklin's Sawmill, Jay noticed a really hot looking car. The car was in front of Papa's truck. It was a small, red, sports car with a long front. Jay asked Papa, "What kind of car is that?" Papa did not know what to say. Papa only saw the manufactured name, Toyota. From the back, the license plate said "JON". Jay and Papa could see a young teenage boy driving. The teenage boy had dark hair. The teenager looked short because he was leaning back on his seat driving. It looked as if he was coming home from college. In the back of the car was luggage and bags. The young man seemed to be very relaxed. Then, all of a sudden, from the left side of the road a very large deer with antlers dashed out in front of the

teenager's car. The deer was very large and rust-colored. It looked as if
it could have been one of Santa's reindeers running away from work.
The large deer had caused the teenage driver to swerve off the road.
The teenage boy could not control the car. Jay and Papa saw the car
heading directly into the ditch. Papa came to a sudden stop on the same
side of the road that the teenager was on. Papa told Jay to stay in the
truck. Papa rushed over from the old, big, blue truck to help the young
man. He asked the young man if he was all right. The teenager said
that he was fine, just shaken up a bit. The deer had run away and it left
damages to the teenager's car. The teenage boy told Papa that his name
was Jonathan Saunders from Florida. Jonathan told Papa that he was on
his way home from NYU College. Papa said to Jonathan that he and Jay
were behind him when he wrecked. Papa told Jonathan that the deer

was large. Papa said, "I am sorry about the damages to your car, that deer really dented your car up bad."

Papa asked Jonathan if he wanted him to take him to the nearest store with a telephone. Jonathan politely said, "Yes, if you do not mind," because he did not have his cell phone with him. Jonathan had forgotten it and left it at the college dorm. Papa took the young man to the nearest store. When they got there the young man called the police. The policeman came and he called the wrecker for Jonathan. Jonathan told Papa thanks and that his parents would be coming to pick him up. Jonathan thanked Papa by shaking Papa's hand for being so nice and helping him. Papa told Jonathan that it was a pleasure to help. Jay and Papa then started looking around in the store for something to snack on for lunch. Papa and Jay both were hungry, so they bought Little Debbie cakes and grape sodas. Jay and Papa got back into the big, old, blue truck and drove on to Franklin's Sawmill. Jay told Papa, "Wow, these seat belts came in great for our sudden stop, didn't they Papa?"

"Yes, you are right," said Papa. Papa said, "We must always be safe and alert when driving. We must always look out for the other person as well as ourselves". Papa told Jay to always remember that when he started driving.

Soon Papa and Jay arrived at Franklin's Sawmill. Papa drove the truck up beside a big, yellow loader. The loader was so large that the sound frightened Jay. The noise sounded like a freight train going by. Jay and Papa got out of the old, big, blue truck. They both stood far away from the truck. The loader had two big mechanical arms in front. The mechanical arms started reaching around the large pile of lumber.

Then the mechanical arms swung the large pile of lumber around to another pile on the ground. The big, yellow loader unloaded the lumber easily. Then Jay and Papa got back into the old, big, blue truck, and went to the office to pick up his check for the load of lumber. Papa had finished all of his business at the sawmill and they started on the return trip home. At the Franklin's Sawmill Jay found answers to all of his fascinating questions. He was feeling quite smart and beginning to learn a little about Papa's business!

Chapter 4

Papa and Jay to the Rescue

Coming closer to home, Jay and Papa saw a lady standing in front of her car. On her head the lady was wearing a large straw hat with yellow, pink, and blue flowers. The sun was very bright, so she wore pink sunglasses for shades. The lady looked like she was going to a picnic in her yellow and green polka dotted dress with the bow in the back. The lady was trying to lift the hood of her car. In the back of her car was a baby in a car seat. Jay could see that the baby was playing with a light blue toy rattle made like a triangle. Jay said, "Papa look, someone else is in trouble! Are we going to stop and help?"

Papa answered, "Yes, we can". When Papa pulled up behind the lady, she was frightened. The lady hopped back into the car. The lady locked all of her car doors and let the windows up. When the lady rolled up both her windows she had only a small opening in each window for her and her baby to breath. But when she saw that Papa and a little boy were getting out of the truck, she relaxed. Jay was smiling and talking with Papa about what could be wrong with the lady's car. When she saw how nice that they both seemed to be, she unlocked the door on the driver's side and let her window down. The lady gently opened up the door and smiled with delight at Jay and Papa. Papa asked the lady if he could help in anyway. The lady told Papa that her name was Mrs. Flowers.

When Mrs. Flowers said her name, Jay thought that it was so funny because her hat had flowers on it, and her perfume was the fragrance of sweet roses in bloom. Mrs. Flowers told Papa that the car just stopped and would not start again.

Mrs. Flowers told Papa that she was on her way to pick up her husband at the airport. She said to Papa that she heard a plunkety plunk sound from under the hood of her car. Papa raised the hood of Mrs. Flowers' car. Papa could see from under the hood that the battery cables had come off of the battery post. Papa had pliers so he tightened the cables back on. While doing this, Papa was thinking back about Jay unscrewing the screw with the wrench as the steam was going up in the air from the old, big, blue truck. Papa hastily fixed Mrs. Flowers

car and started it up, it sounded very good. Papa told Mrs. Flowers that she should not have any more problems with it. Mrs Flowers felt very grateful to Papa for helping her with the car. She offered Papa money in appreciation for his kindness. But Papa would not take the money, he was just happy that he could help. Mrs. Flowers thanked Papa, and waved good-bye to Jay as she drove off. Jay was thinking that his Papa was the "best-ist" Papa in the whole world!

Chapter 5

Grandma's Home Cooking

Papa finally pulled into the driveway. Jay and Papa were feeling very happy. Jay was happy that Papa had fixed the screw that he had loosened up with the wrench and proud of his Papa for helping Jonathan, the teenager, and the lady, Mrs. Flowers with her baby.

Grandma was also happy to see Jay and Papa. Grandma had been waiting most of the day for them to return home. She told them to go inside and wash their hands. Grandma had cooked collard greens, candied yams, fried chicken and hot rolls. Jay's stomach was growling just by passing the kitchen door. The aroma was high in the

air. Grandma's fried chicken was so good that it melted off the bone into your mouth when you picked it up. For dessert, Jay and Papa had hot apple pie, and ice cream. Grandma had cooked all of their favorite foods. Jay had eaten so much of Grandma's tasty food that he had to unsnap the button on his jeans. Jay and Papa had eaten a gigantic meal. Jay said to his Grandma, "Grandma, my Momma is a good cook, but Grandma, you've got Momma beat!" Grandma smiled and said to Jay that he will never go hungry at Grandma's house, Jay walked off feeling pleased with his Grandma.

Jay enjoyed the long trip from Franklin's Sawmill.

Papa saw that he still had a little more time before darkness fell, so he went out to wrap up some small jobs before it was to late.

Chapter 6

Mr. Elton's Farm

The next day, early in the afternoon, Jay and Papa got back into the old, big, blue truck. Jay and Papa went down to Papa's sawmill. Papa said that he had to take a neighbor some sawdust for his farm. The neighbor's name was Mr. Elton. Papa started placing the upright planks that he had nailed together on each side of the truck. The planks were to keep the sawdust from falling off the sides of the truck while carrying it. Papa started loading the sawdust for Mr. Elton's farm with his tractor. Papa scooped one load onto the truck and then two loads onto the truck. Papa scooped up enough sawdust to fill the whole back

of the truck. Papa then covered the back of the truck with a large blue plastic sheet. Papa did not want the sawdust to blow off the truck while driving to Mr. Elton's farm. Papa drove over to Mr. Elton's house a mile down the road. Mr. Elton was a farmer who had blue eyes and blondish hair. He wore a rough looking blue cap. On Mr. Elton's cap were the word GOODYEAR Tires on the front. In the conversation with Papa he said that he loved collecting model cars and quite a few junk cars too. Mr. Elton had farm animals like cows, horses, pigs and chickens. Seeing the animals was fine for Jay but the smell was awful. Mr. Elton told Papa to dump the sawdust for bedding his horses on the farm and for his other animals by the horses shed. Mr. Elton thanked Papa for delivering the sawdust and told Papa that he would be asking for more in about three months for his farm.

Chapter 7

Going to the Rock Quarry

Papa decided next to go to the rock quarry. Papa said that he needed gravel for the driveway. The quarry was not far from Mr. Elton's farm. Jay and Papa made it just in time before the quarry closed. Papa pulled up to the big gravel loader. The gravel loader was big and yellow. The loader had a large bucket on the back. The loader also had very large forks on the front. All of a sudden, all of the gravel fell right into the bed of the old, big, blue truck. The truck sunk down like air being pushed from a bouncing ball. Jay said "Ooooh that was fun." He liked the feeling of the old, big, blue truck sinking down. The truck was sinking down as the

gravel was falling from the loader. Before the gravel finished falling, Jay heard a horn. The horn meant to stop the gravel. The truck had filled up. Papa drove up to the payment window and paid the attendant.

Papa drove back home and he slowly raised the bed of the old, big, blue truck and let the gravel fall. Papa started at the top of the driveway. He let Jay help to operate the steering wheel. Papa placed his large hands over Jay's small hands. He helped Jay to guide the steering wheel, while the truck moved slowly down from the driveway releasing the gravel. Slowly the gravel fell onto Papa's driveway until they were finished. Then Papa and Jay raked the gravel. There were big gravel and little gravel. They all served a purpose for their sizes.

Chapter 8

A Time To Relax

Papa was starting to wind down now from all of the work he had done, so he told Jay, "Let's go fishing." Jay answered Papa, "Fishing, all right!" Fishing was one of Jay's most favorite sports of the year. Papa had a friend whose name was Mr. Turner. Mr. Turner did not mind Papa fishing in his pond. Mr. Turner always told Papa that whenever he wanted to fish in his pond that it was "ok" with him. Papa knew that Jay would enjoy fishing. To Jay, just watching all kinds of fish swim by was exciting. Mr. Turner's pond was ten minutes from his house. Papa drove the old, big, blue truck from Mr. Turner's house to Mr. Turner's fishing pond with Jay right by his side. When Jay and Papa arrived, Jay jumped out and went to the back of the old, big, blue truck to get a shovel to dig for the worms. Jay was so excited about going fishing with Papa. Jay loved the smell of digging into the moist earth. When Jay and Papa had finished digging for worms, they both went on their way walking a little ways to the fishing bank. The pond was very clean. Anyone could stand around Mr. Turner's pond to fish and not be in any high weeds. Jay pitched his fishing line into the water and it was not long before Jay had caught the biggest fish in the pond! Jay had caught a large bass. Jay removed the hook from the fish's mouth and put the fish into the bucket of cold water to keep the fish fresh. Papa was so amazed that he hugged Jay, and congratulated him for such a great job. Papa reached for his camera and took Jay's picture. Jay held the fish so high in the air to make sure Papa got a good snapshot of him smiling and holding up the large fish. Papa did not have much time to catch anything because it was getting late. After Jay and Papa had finished fishing, they were ready to release the large fish back into the pond.

As Jay was about to pitch the fish back, Jay came too close to the edge of the fish pond bank. Jay's foot slipped and he accidentally fell into the pond. Jay shouted out to Papa, "Help"! Jay splashed in the water, trying to get back to Papa on the fishing bank. Papa immediately cut a long tree limb and reached for Jay. Papa told Jay to grab hold to the limb while he pulled him in safely to the fishing bank. Papa pulled Jay in and Jay was wet from the top of his head to the bottom of his feet. Papa told Jay to take off his shirt and wring the shirt out, and try to get as much water from his pants and shoes as he could. Papa found a piece of cardboard from behind the truck seat and told Jay to sit on it. Jay was so wet and soggy that Papa packed up their fishing gear and got ready to leave. Jay told Papa that the next time they go fishing the fish stays with them, instead of him swimming with it down stream! Jay and Papa laughed, and said, what a exciting time this has been!

Papa and Jay got into the old, big, blue truck and returned home.

Chapter 9
A Visit to Great-Grandma Len's

Before going to bed, Papa thought about going to see Great-Grandma Len in the old, big, blue truck. Papa wanted to see if his Mom needed anything before he turned in for the night. Great-Grandma Len was old and disabled. She could not walk like Jay and Papa. Great-Grandma was in a wheelchair. Great-Grandma had lost her legs because of diabetes. Her sight was also bad. Great-Grandma Len lived with her two sons Henry and David who took very good care of her. But Great-Grandma Len did not want anyone to pity her. Great-Grandma Len always said that she would be "Ok".

A care-taker always came by to help Great-Grandma Len everyday. Great-Grandma Len called her Debbie. Debbie would help Great-Grandma to exercise and how to make her bed, along with other activities. Debbie took really good care of Great-Grandma Len.

Great-Grandma Len always received calls from her friends telling her about that day's events. Jay loved his Great-Grandma, and Great-Grandma loved him and all of her great grandchildren. The youngest of all was Carlashia. Carlashia visited Great-Grandma Len every time her father would bring her down. Great-Grandma Len had nine great grandchildren in all, and she enjoyed them all.

Sundays was a treat for Great-Grandma Len. Papa would always bring Great-Grandma something special to eat. Papa would go to an "all you can eat" restaurant after church and buy her lunch. Most of the

time Papa bought Great-Grandma Len baked fish, peas, cabbage, and corn on the cob. When Papa delivered Great-Grandma Len's Sunday meals, She would start talking about many things that she did or did not do in her life. Although she did not go anywhere, Great-Grandma could tell you about anything going on in the neighborhood. she knew just about everything before Papa and Grandma by having a telephone and a radio in her house. Grandma would hear it first, and then give them the scoop when they came to see her. This helped Great-Grandma Len to keep busy and have something to do besides just sitting in her wheelchair day by day.

Now that it was almost nine-o-clock and getting late, it was bedtime for Jay. Papa was ready to go back home to prepare for tomorrow's chores. Great Grandma Len waved good-by to Jay and said good-by to

Papa. Great Grandma told Jay to come back and spend more time with her before he returned home to the city. Jay told Great Grandma Len that he would be back tomorrow if Papa comes back.

Papa drove back to the house before Jay got too sleepy to walk, Jay was tuckered out.

Chapter 10

Jay Plans His Future

Jay went upstairs to take his bath. He said goodnight to his Papa and Grandma. After that he said his prayers, and leaped into his nice, comfortable bed that Grandma had prepared for him. Jay had such an exciting time with Papa. He could not believe all that had happened. Jay told Papa that since he had arrived he has had so much fun. This all started with the skunk being in the shed and to him falling in the fishpond. "I know there is much more excitement to come," said Jay, because summer is not over yet. Jay thanked God for such a wonderful time with his Papa and Grandma.

Jay's Grandma and Papa knelt down to kiss him on his forehead, and said, "Goodnight."

As soon as Jay's head touched his nice soft pillow he closed his eyes. He started dreaming a very special dream about his future. He dreamed that he was smart just like Papa. He also dreamed that he was the owner of his own lumber business. Jay went as far as naming the business, "Jay's Lumber Company". In Jay's dream, he was delivering lumber. He was delivering lumber to a mill for furniture to be made. What was so exciting about this dream was, Jay was driving Papa in Jay's old, big, blue truck, with the business name "Jay's Lumber Company" in very large printed letters on both side of the truck doors. What a fantastic dream!

Printed in the United States
by Baker & Taylor Publisher Services